Dear parents, caregivers, and educators:

If you want to get your child excited about reading, you've come to the right place! Ready-to-Read *GRAPHICS* is the perfect launchpad for emerging graphic novel readers.

All Ready-to-Read *GRAPHICS* books include the following:

- ★ **A how-to guide to reading graphic novels for first-time readers**

- ★ **Easy-to-follow panels to support reading comprehension**

- ★ **Accessible vocabulary to build your child's reading confidence**

- ★ **Compelling stories that star your child's favorite characters**

- ★ **Fresh, engaging illustrations that provide context and promote visual literacy**

Wherever your child may be on their reading journey, Ready-to-Read *GRAPHICS* will make them giggle, gasp, and want to keep reading more.

Blast off on this starry adventure . . . a universe of graphic novel reading awaits!

Geraldine Pu and Her Lucky Pencil, Too!

Written and illustrated by Maggie P. Chang

Ready-to-Read GRAPHICS

Simon Spotlight

New York   London   Toronto   Sydney   New Delhi

For my mother

Thank you to Isabel Marte for assisting me in the coloring of this book.

SIMON SPOTLIGHT
An imprint of Simon & Schuster Children's Publishing Division
1230 Avenue of the Americas, New York, New York 10020
This Simon Spotlight edition August 2022
Copyright © 2022 by Margaret Chang
All rights reserved, including the right of reproduction in whole or in part in any form.
SIMON SPOTLIGHT, READY-TO-READ, and colophon are registered
trademarks of Simon & Schuster, Inc.
For information about special discounts for bulk purchases, please contact
Simon & Schuster Special Sales at 1-866-506-1949 or business@simonandschuster.com.
Manufactured in the United States of America 0722 LAK
2 4 6 8 10 9 7 5 3 1
Library of Congress Cataloging-in-Publication Data
Names: Chang, Maggie P., author, illustrator. Title: Geraldine Pu and her lucky pencil, too!/
written and illustrated by Maggie P. Chang. Description: Simon Spotlight edition. |
New York : Simon Spotlight, 2022. | Series: Geraldine Pu | Summary: "Geraldine Pu is
assigned to write a true story about her family at school and discovers that her family is full
of incredible memories"— Provided by publisher. Identifiers: LCCN 2022011530 (print) |
LCCN 2022011531 (ebook) | ISBN 9781534484757 (hardcover) | ISBN 9781534484740
(paperback) | ISBN 9781534484764 (ebook) Subjects: CYAC: Graphic novels. |
Storytelling—Fiction. | Schools—Fiction. | Families—Fiction. | Taiwanese Americans—Fiction. |
LCGFT: Graphic novels. Classification: LCC PZ7.7.C419 Gdu 2022 (print) |
LCC PZ7.7.C419 (ebook) | DDC 741.5/973—dc23/eng/20220502
LC record available at https://lccn.loc.gov/2022011530
LC ebook record available at https://lccn.loc.gov/2022011531

Contents

How to Read This Book

This is Geraldine. She's here to give you some tips on reading this book.

It's me, Geraldine! The pointy end of this speech bubble shows that I'm speaking.

When someone is thinking, you'll see a bubbly cloud with little circles pointing to them.

This box I'm inside is called a panel. On each page, read the panels from left to right...

...and top to bottom.

Ta-da! Now you're READY TO READ this book!

GURGLE GURGLE

Oops, those gurgles were the sound of my tummy grumbling. It's time to eat!

HEE-HEE

Words from Geraldine's World

Geraldine and her family speak English, Mandarin Chinese, and Taiwanese. Mandarin Chinese and Taiwanese are both languages spoken in Taiwan. Some of Geraldine's family members used to live there!

 Amah (said like this: ah-MAH): the word for "Grandma" in Taiwanese.

Chienbee (said like this: chee-EN-bee): the word for "pencil" in Mandarin Chinese.

 Chinese ribbon dance: a traditional art form from China that's been performed for over 1,000 years. These dancers wear colorful costumes and whirl long strips of silk in the air.

karaoke (said like this: keh-REE-OH-KEE): a fun, musical activity where people sing along to music videos while using a microphone.

potluck: a get-together where people bring food to share.

A note on the spellings in this book:
There are different ways to write Mandarin Chinese and Taiwanese words in the English alphabet, but our book spells them the way Geraldine likes to spell them.

Chapter One

Meet Geraldine Pu. Her last name rhymes with "glue" and "drew."

She loves her family,

her favorite things,

hair clip

Amah's cooking

art supplies

and stories with mystery and adventure.

The stories Geraldine
loves the most are...

...the ones she comes up with herself!

In a flash, lightning strikes the magic horse's wing!

Oh no! It can't fly!

The knight and her horse fall toward...

Do you know what always helps Geraldine
with her stories?

Her lucky pencil.

ME!

Geraldine calls him Chienbee (said like this: chee-EN-bee).

He writes and draws what's in Geraldine's imagination.

Then a swarm of fairies comes to the rescue!

Wheee!

Wait, that doesn't look right.

Chienbee also has a cool eraser.

Every time she picks him up, she has great ideas for her stories. That's why he's her lucky pencil.

One day at school, Mr. Lunder announces,

Each student picks a different
story idea from a bag.

Geraldine is excited until...

...she picks: →

MY FAMILY

Hmm...

Even though she loves her family, she can't think of any exciting stories about them.

Soon, everyone gets to work,
except Geraldine.

After a while, Mr. Lunder says,

Geraldine finds her name under...

She has two days to come up with a brilliant story.

Hey, I'm not a chew toy! Ow!

Chapter Two

The next morning Geraldine plays tic-tac-toe with Deven on the bus.

So, what are you writing about for your story?

Once, a pigeon flew into my house, and my mom chased it, and my baby sister cried, and I hid, and my dad took pictures, and feathers went EVERYWHERE.

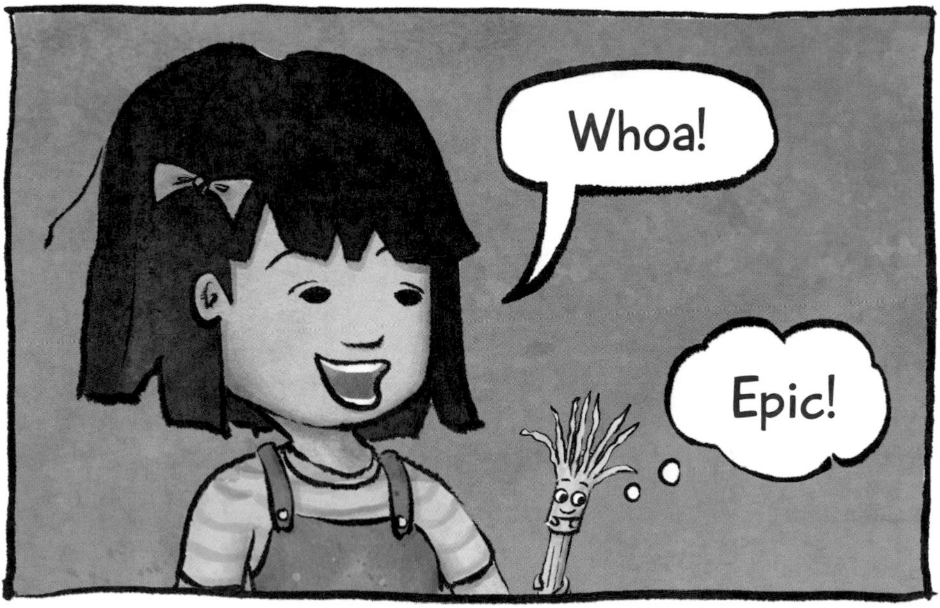
Whoa!
Epic!

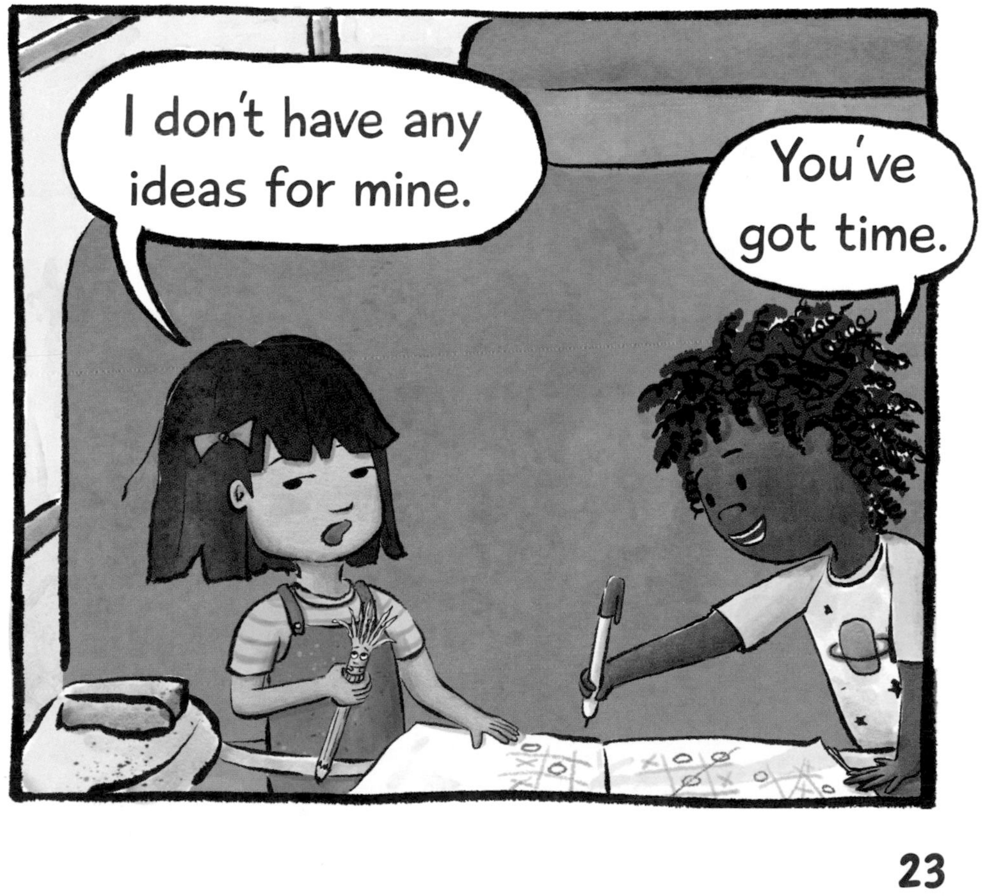
I don't have any ideas for mine.
You've got time.

Later Geraldine's class begins presenting.

Geraldine has one more day to write,
but she barely touches Chienbee.

At home Geraldine knows she has to work on her story. Instead, she does a few other things first.

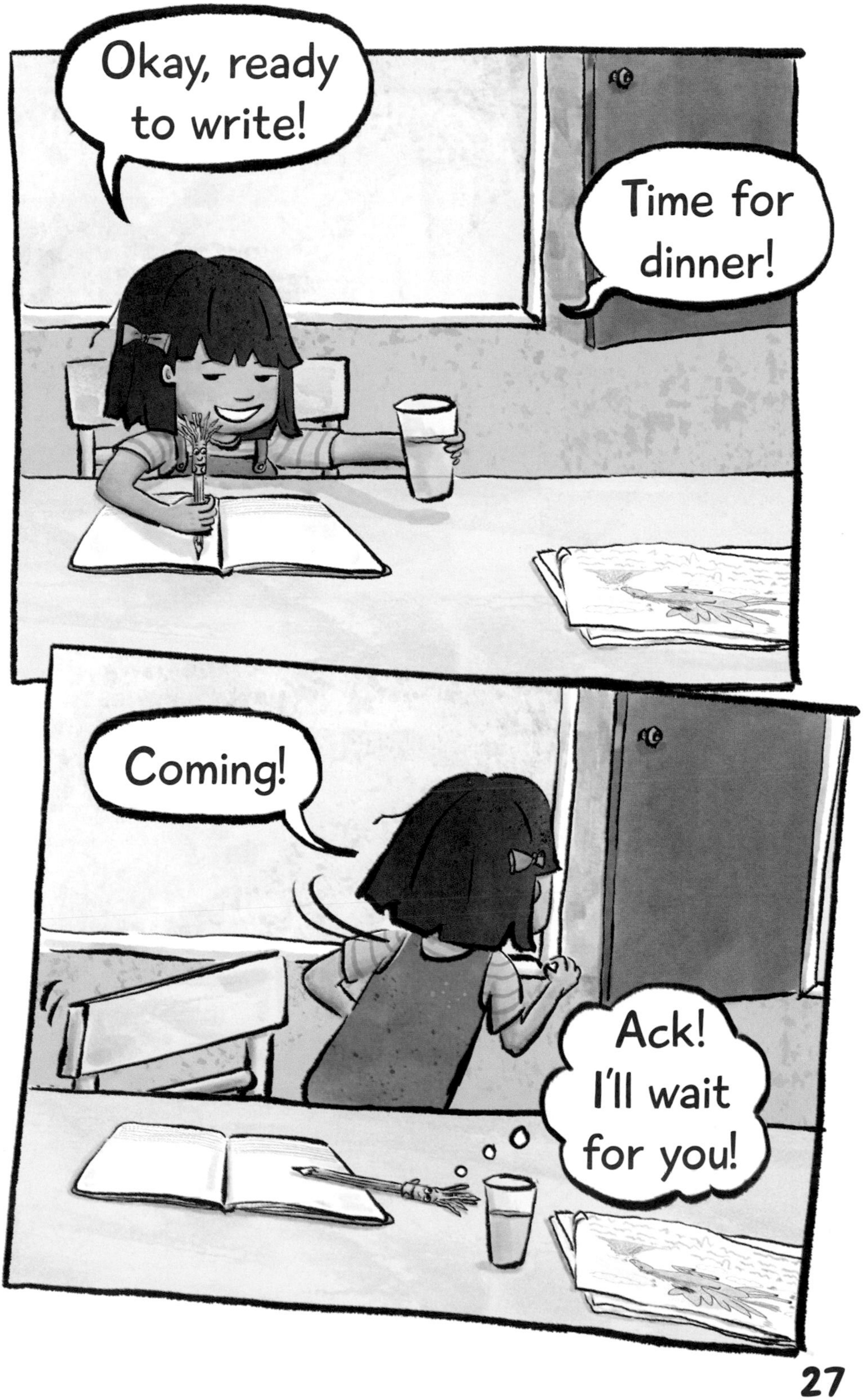
Okay, ready to write!
Time for dinner!
Coming!
Ack! I'll wait for you!

After dinner Geraldine tries to focus.

But mostly she uses Chienbee's eraser...

Then she starts doing this...

Until finally...

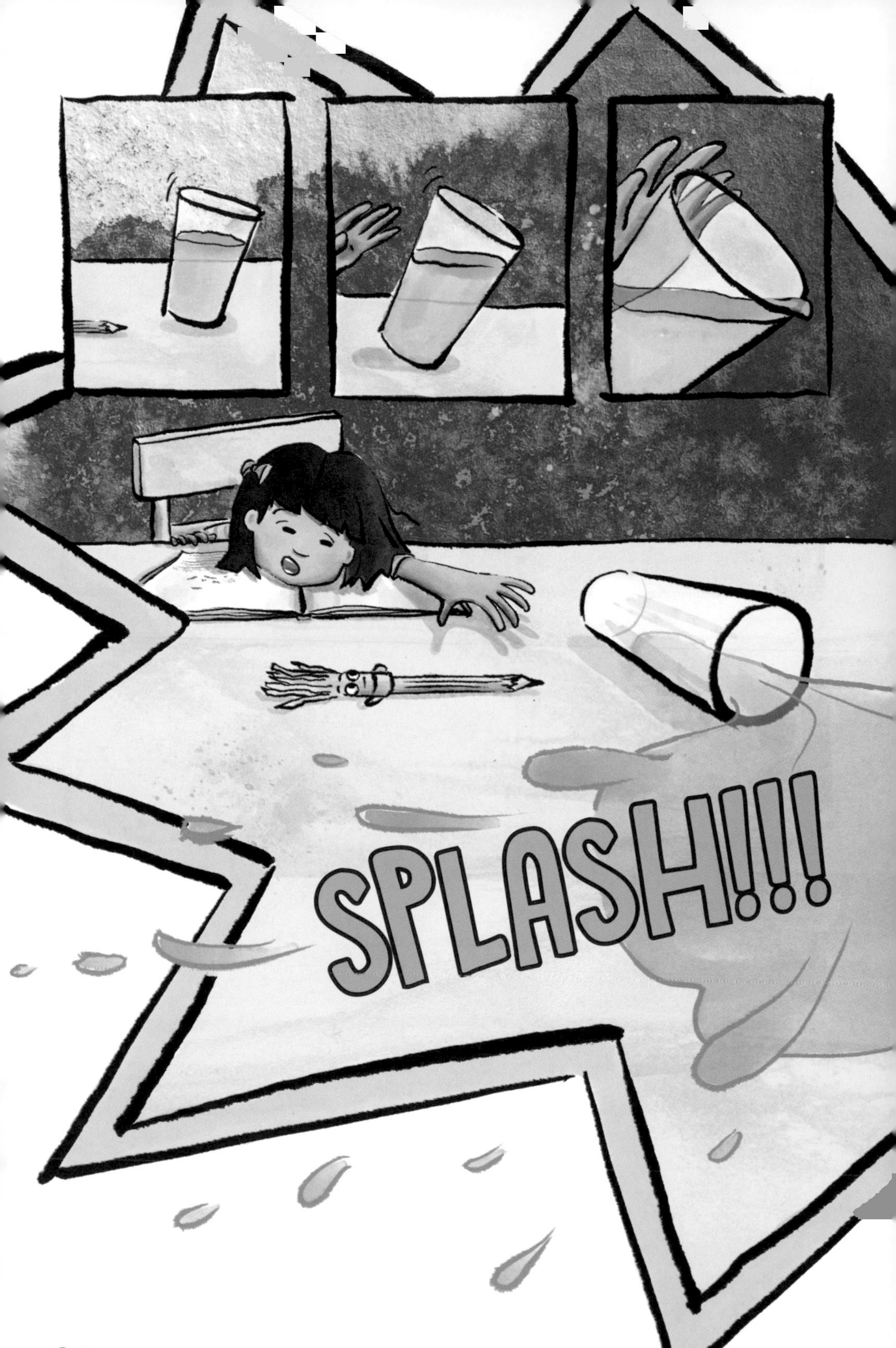
SPLASH!!!!

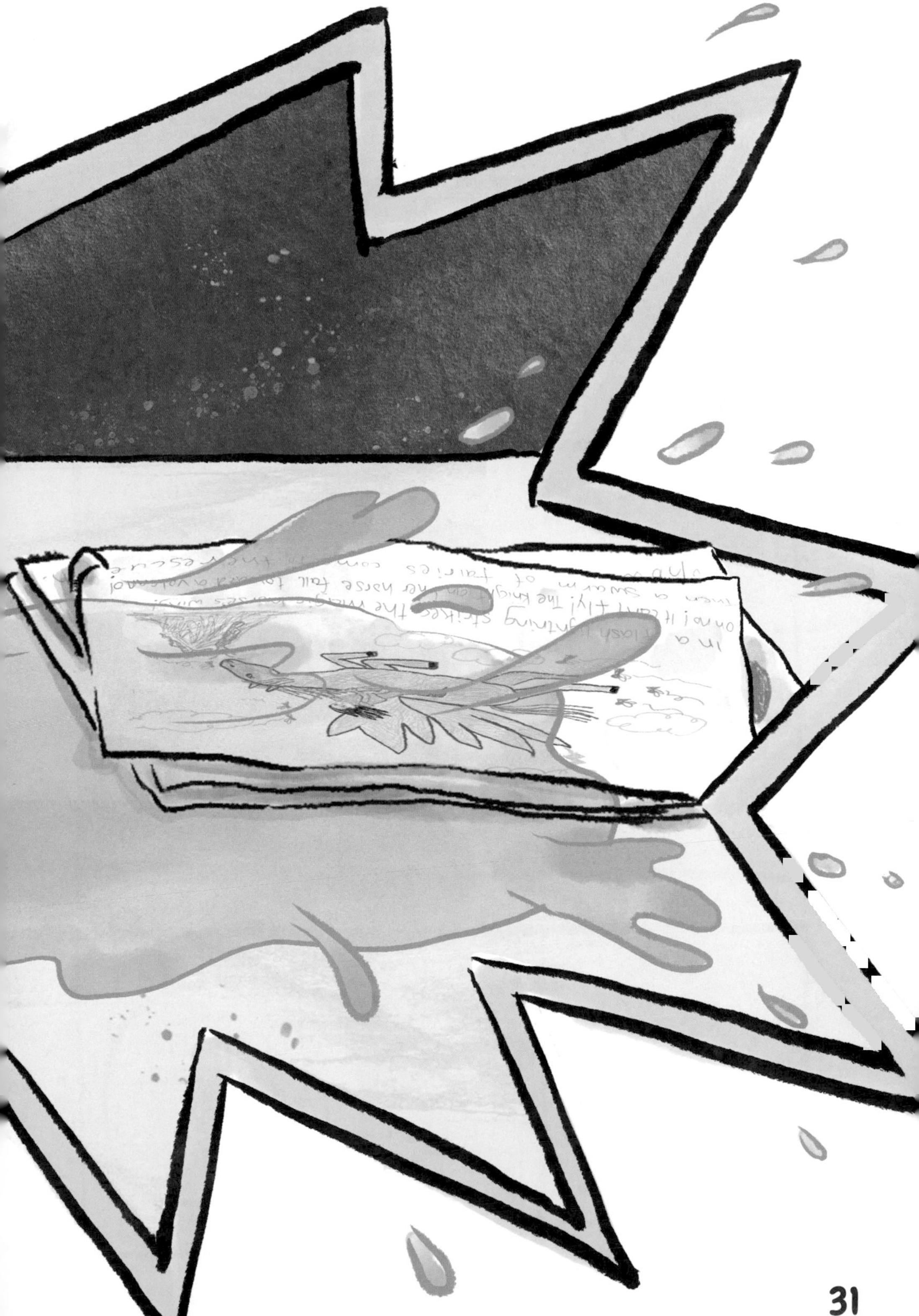

Nooo!

Geraldine's magic horse story is soaked.

She sighs,

You're not so lucky, after all.

DRIP

Geraldine, what happened?

Geraldine explains her project.

Chapter Three

Come with me.

Amah heads to the basement.

The basement is mysterious.

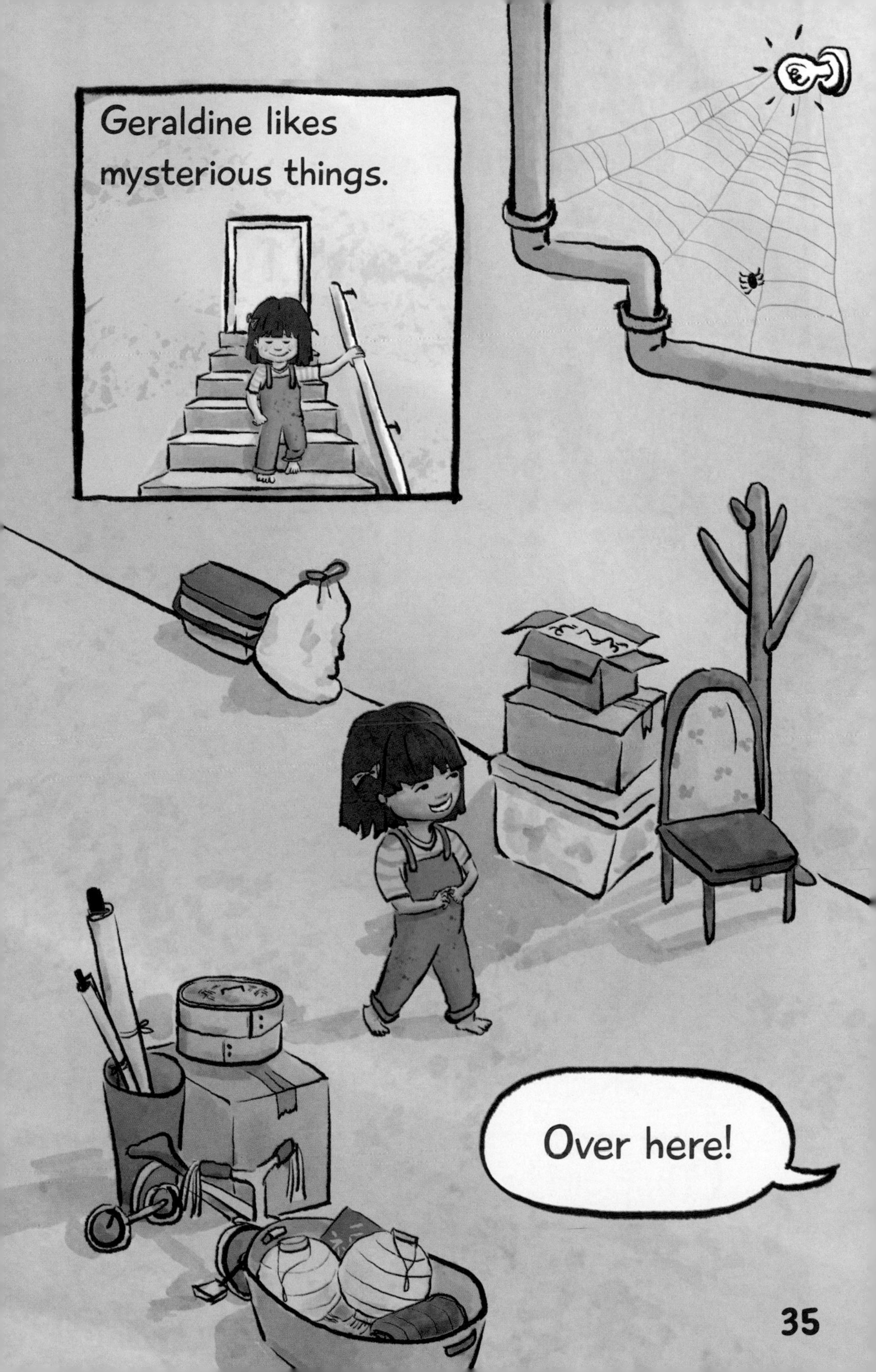
Geraldine likes
mysterious things.
Over here!

Amah shows Geraldine a photo of where she used to live in Taiwan,

and the plane she took when she
moved to the United States.

There is even a photo of young Amah dancing a Chinese ribbon dance.

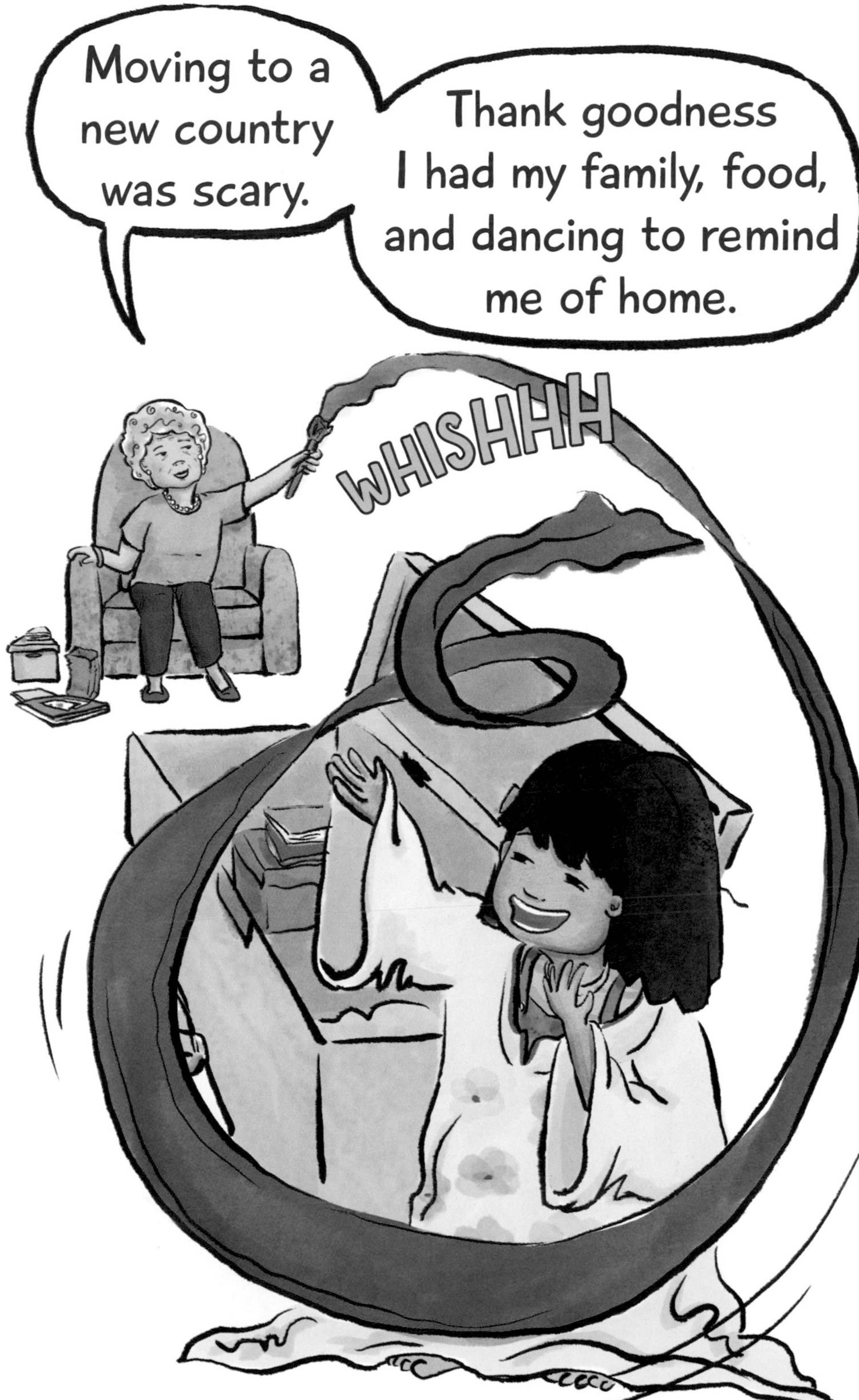
Moving to a new country was scary.
Thank goodness I had my family, food, and dancing to remind me of home.
WHISHHH

Amah tells stories of her dance group,

of how Geraldine's parents met,

and of the night Geraldine was born.

The moon was like magic.

By the time the trunk is empty, Geraldine says,

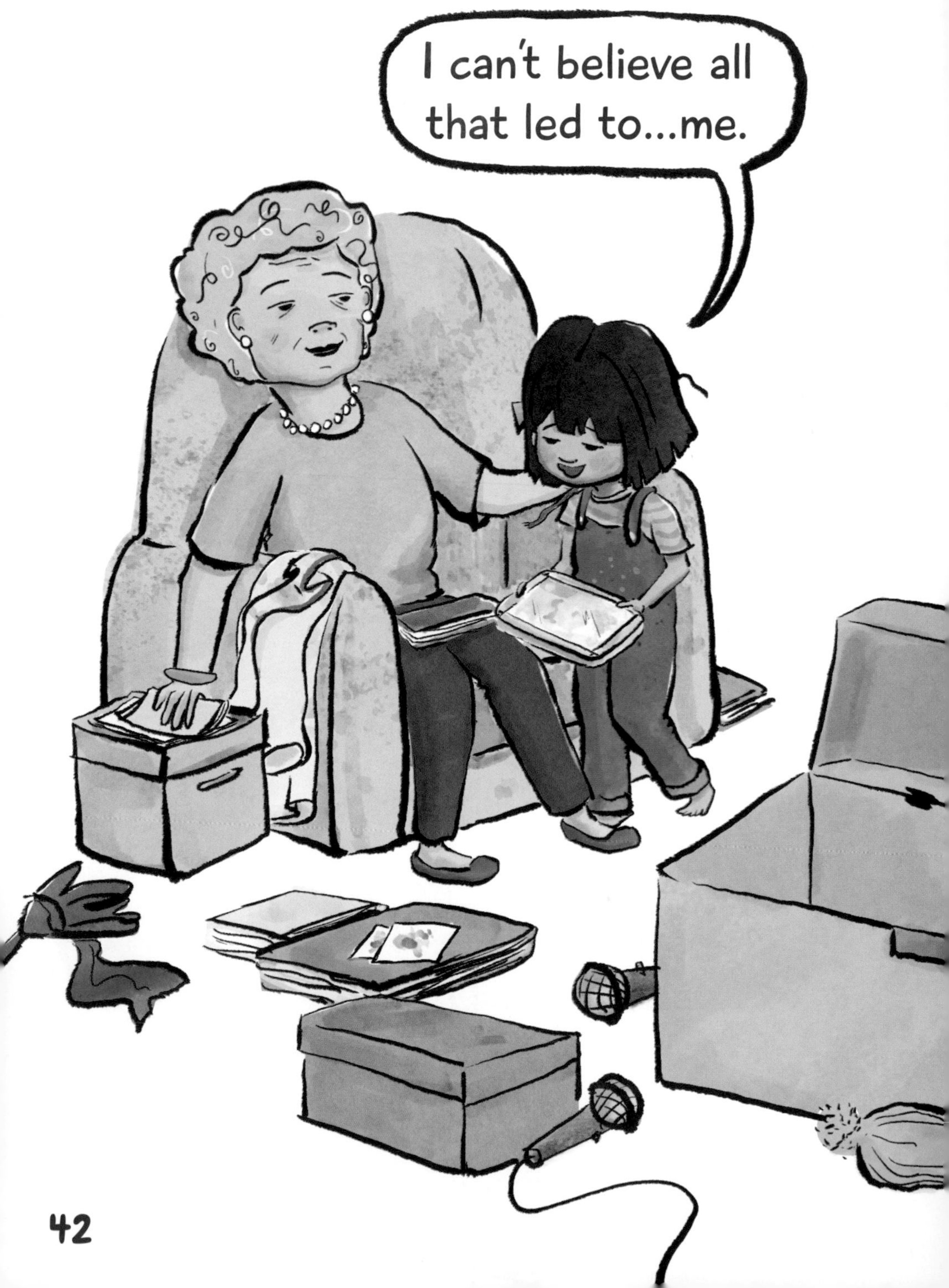
I can't believe all that led to...me.

Hey! Amah, I know what to write!

Can I have this ribbon?

Sure.

Thank you!

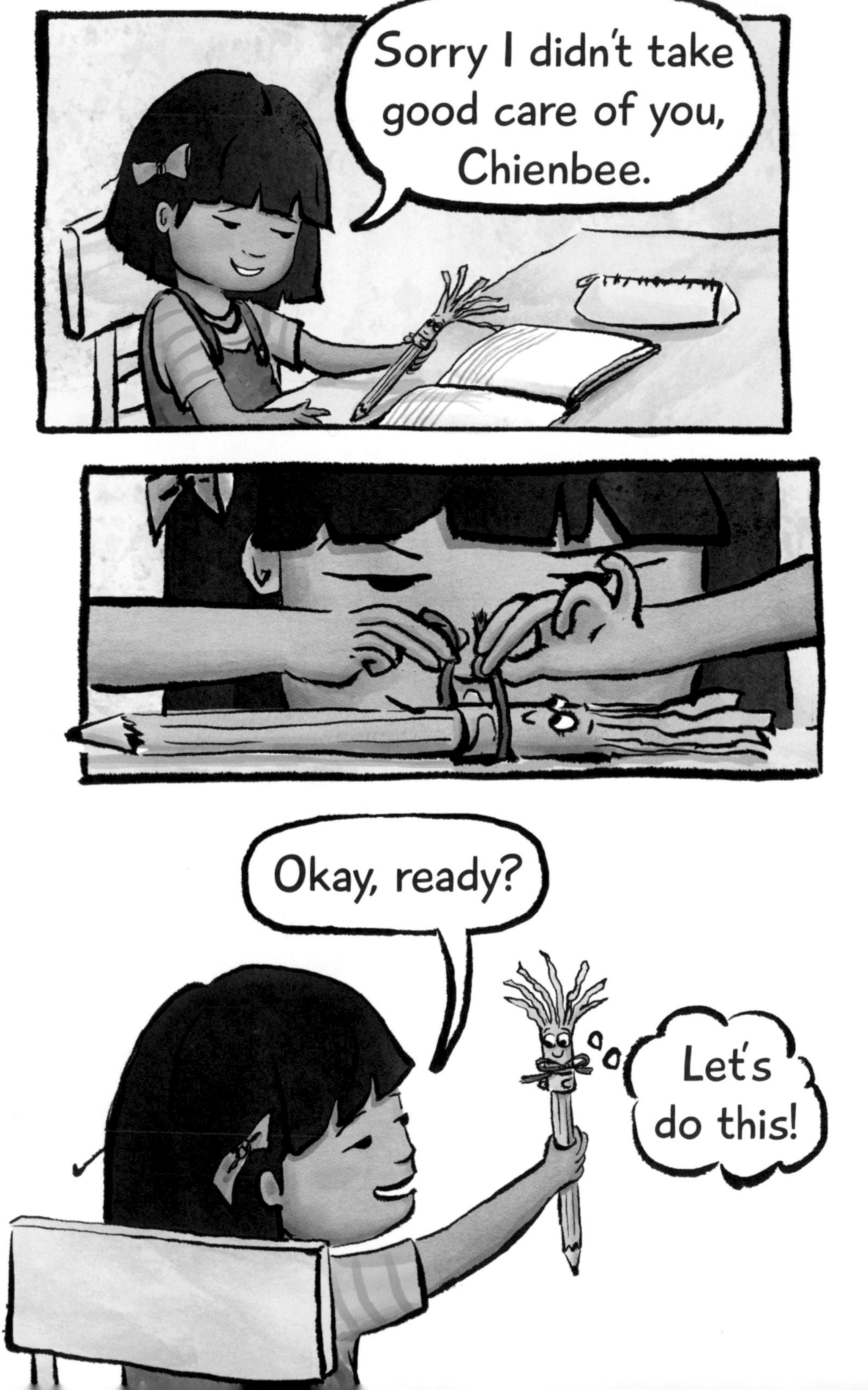
Sorry I didn't take good care of you, Chienbee.
Okay, ready?
Let's do this!

SWISH
SWISH SCRATCH
SCRIBBLE
SCRATCH
SCRIBBLE SCRIBBLE
SWISH SCRATCH

DONE!

The next day is Wednesday.

Geraldine practices reading her story
to Auggie,

then eats a big breakfast.

Before she knows it, school starts and...

Chapter Four

Geraldine flips through her notebook.

Oh my dear, your palms are sweaty!

She looks into the crowd.

Everyone stares back.

She opens her mouth,

but suddenly out comes a...

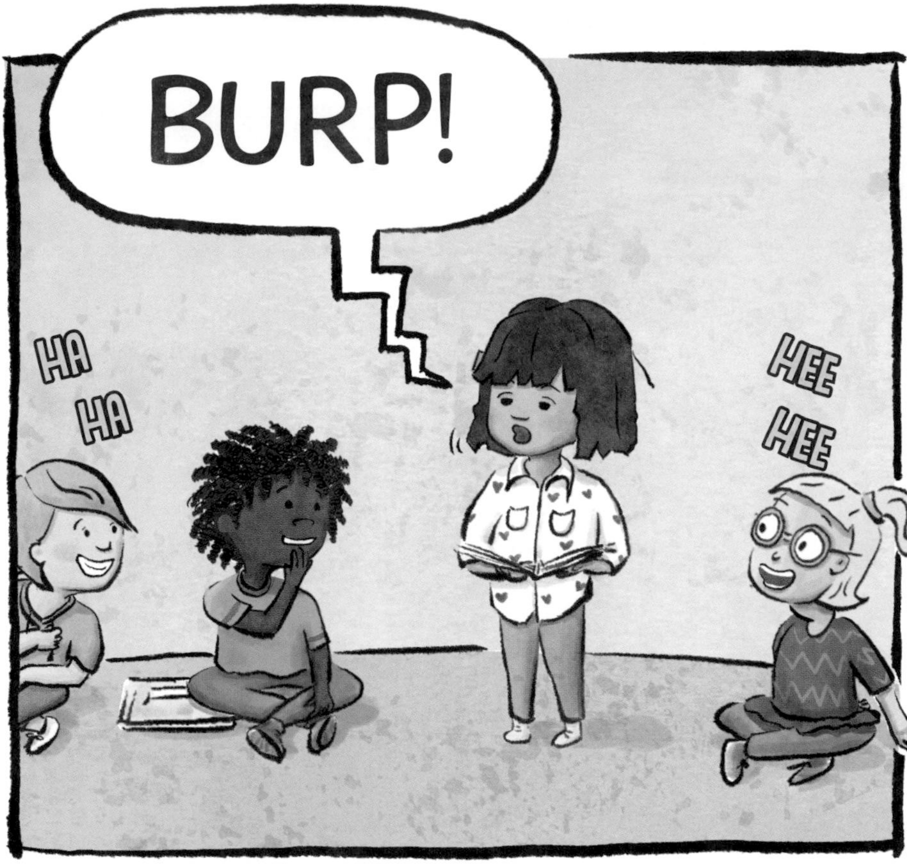
BURP!
HA HA
HEE HEE

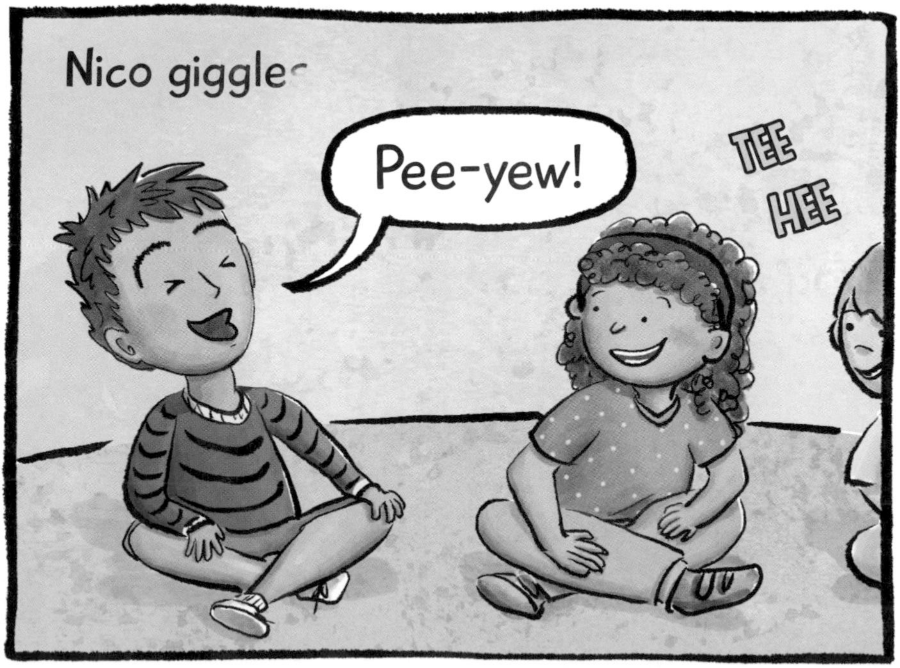
Nico giggle
Pee-yew!
TEE HEE

Now, now, class.

Geraldine is giggling, too, though.

Excuse me! Pee-yew is right!

P-U is also how you spell Pu—my family's name.

Speaking of my family...

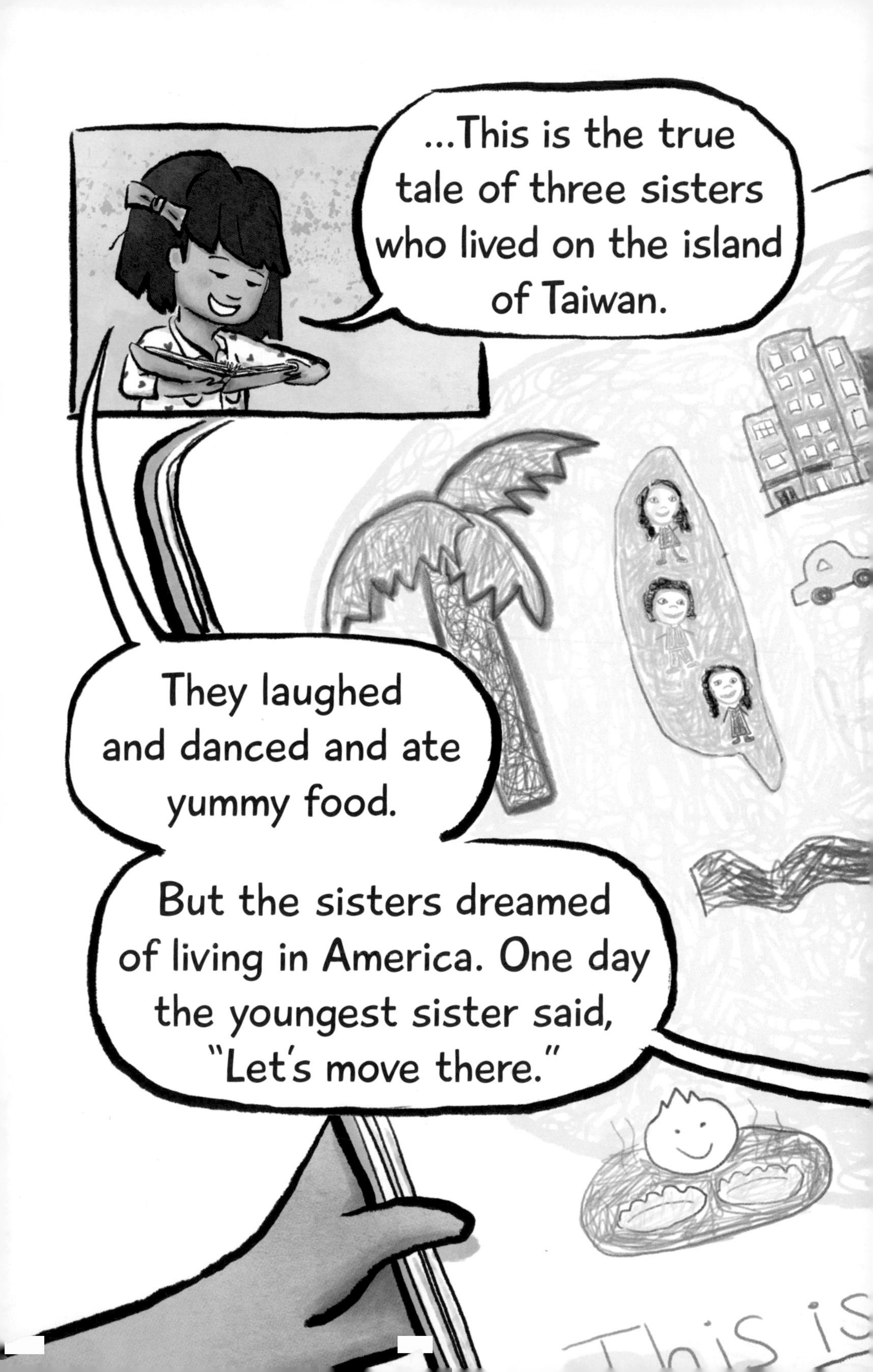
...This is the true tale of three sisters who lived on the island of Taiwan.
They laughed and danced and ate yummy food.
But the sisters dreamed of living in America. One day the youngest sister said, "Let's move there."
This is

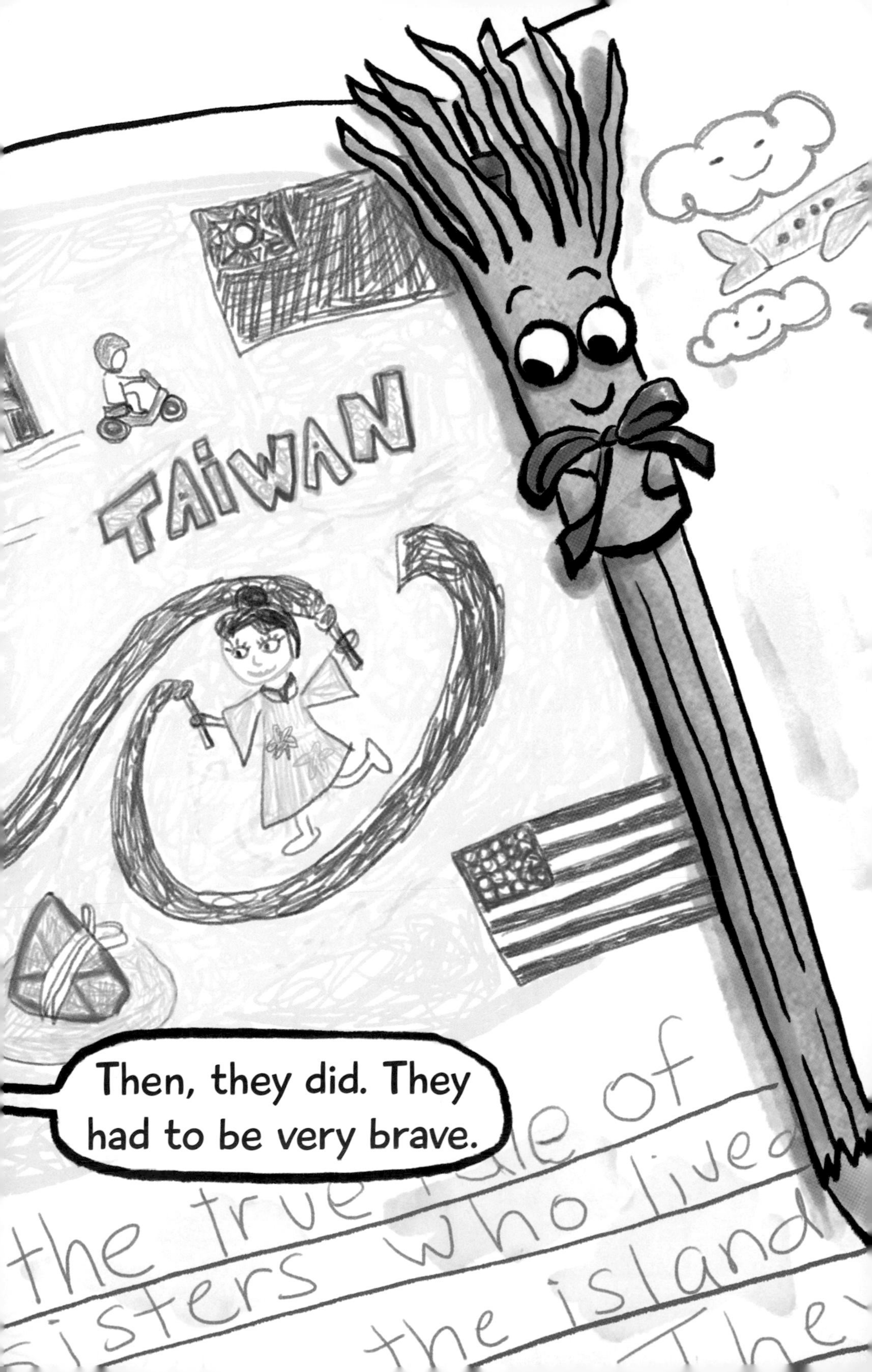
TAIWAN
Then, they did. They had to be very brave.
the true tale of
sisters who lived
the island
They

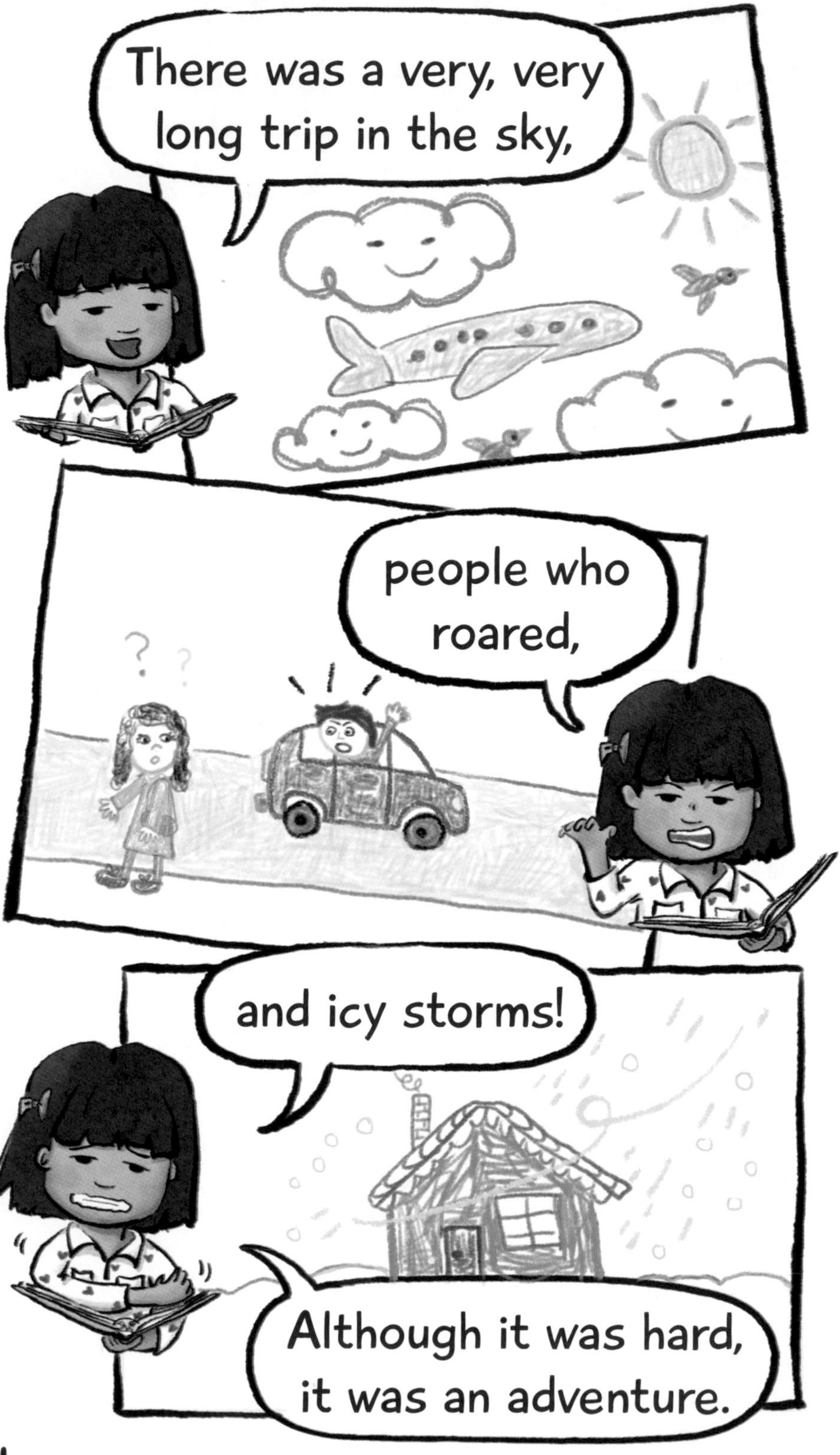
There was a very, very long trip in the sky,
people who roared,
and icy storms!
Although it was hard, it was an adventure.

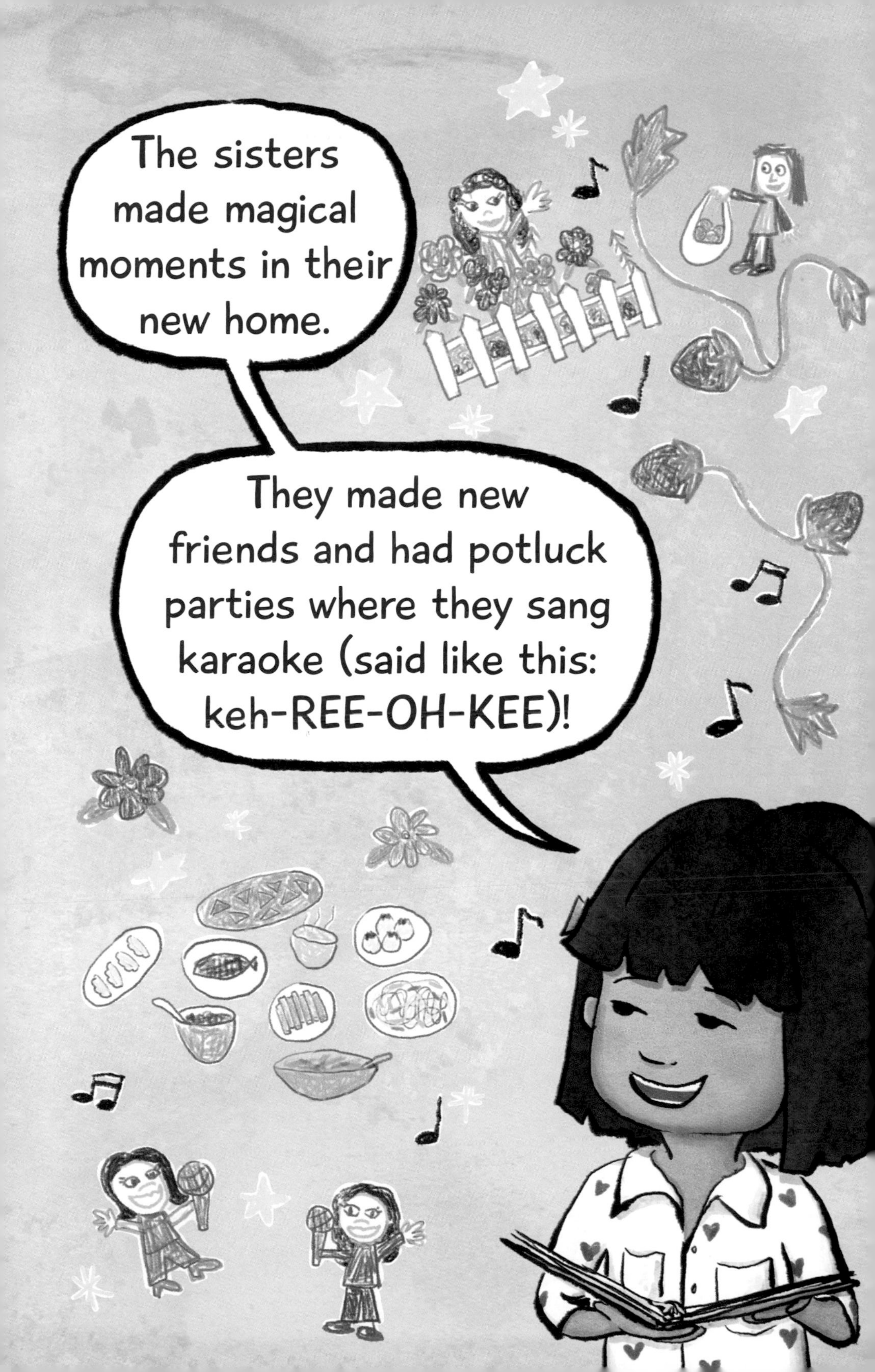
The sisters made magical moments in their new home.
They made new friends and had potluck parties where they sang karaoke (said like this: keh-REE-OH-KEE)!

Now, for a big reveal.

The youngest sister in this story is my Amah—my grandma!

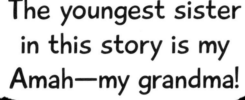

Awww!

And I love being her granddaughter. The end!

The class is silent.

Then someone starts clapping.

CLAP
CLAP

Soon...

...everyone's cheering!

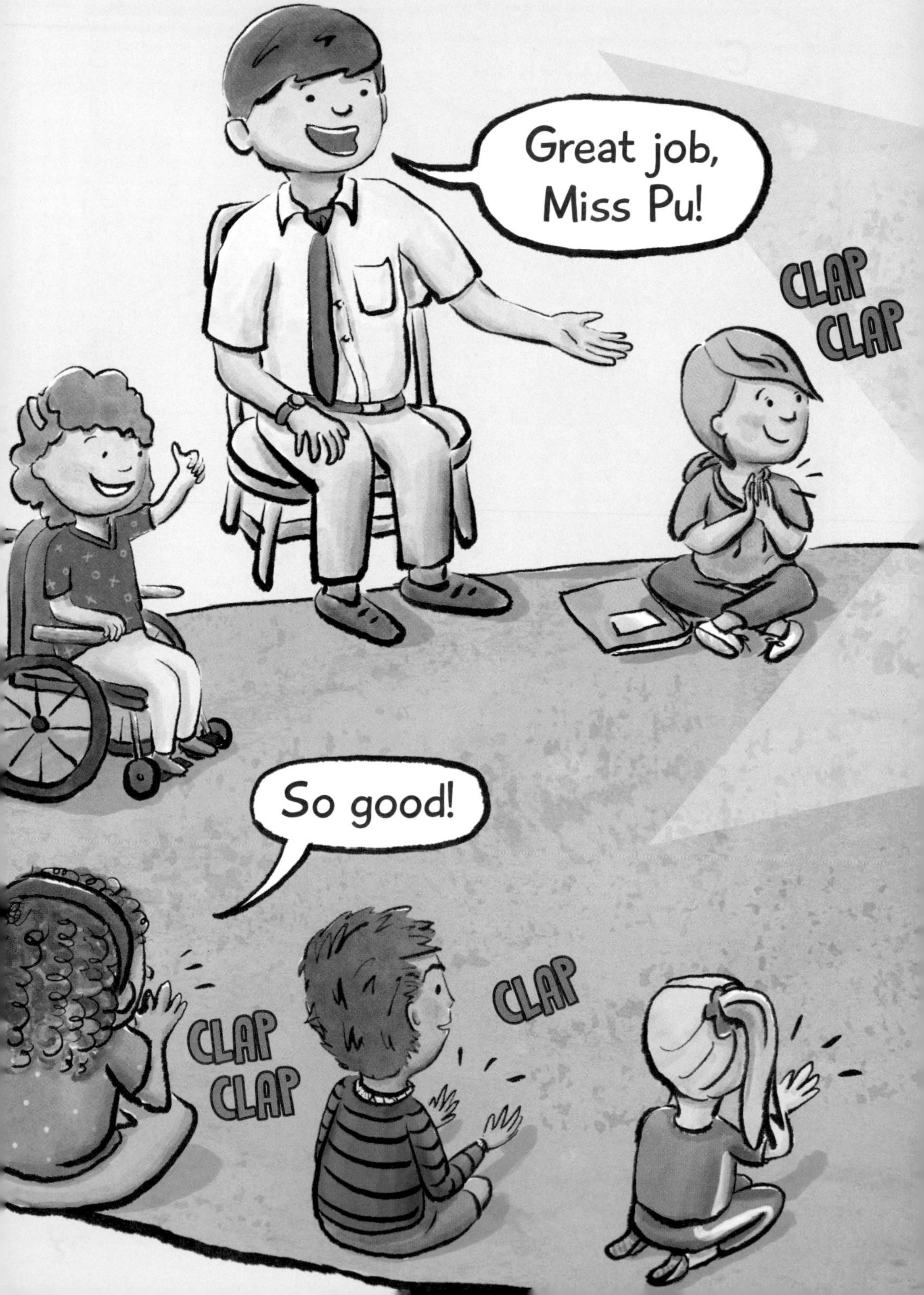
Great job, Miss Pu!
CLAP
CLAP
So good!
CLAP
CLAP
CLAP
CLAP

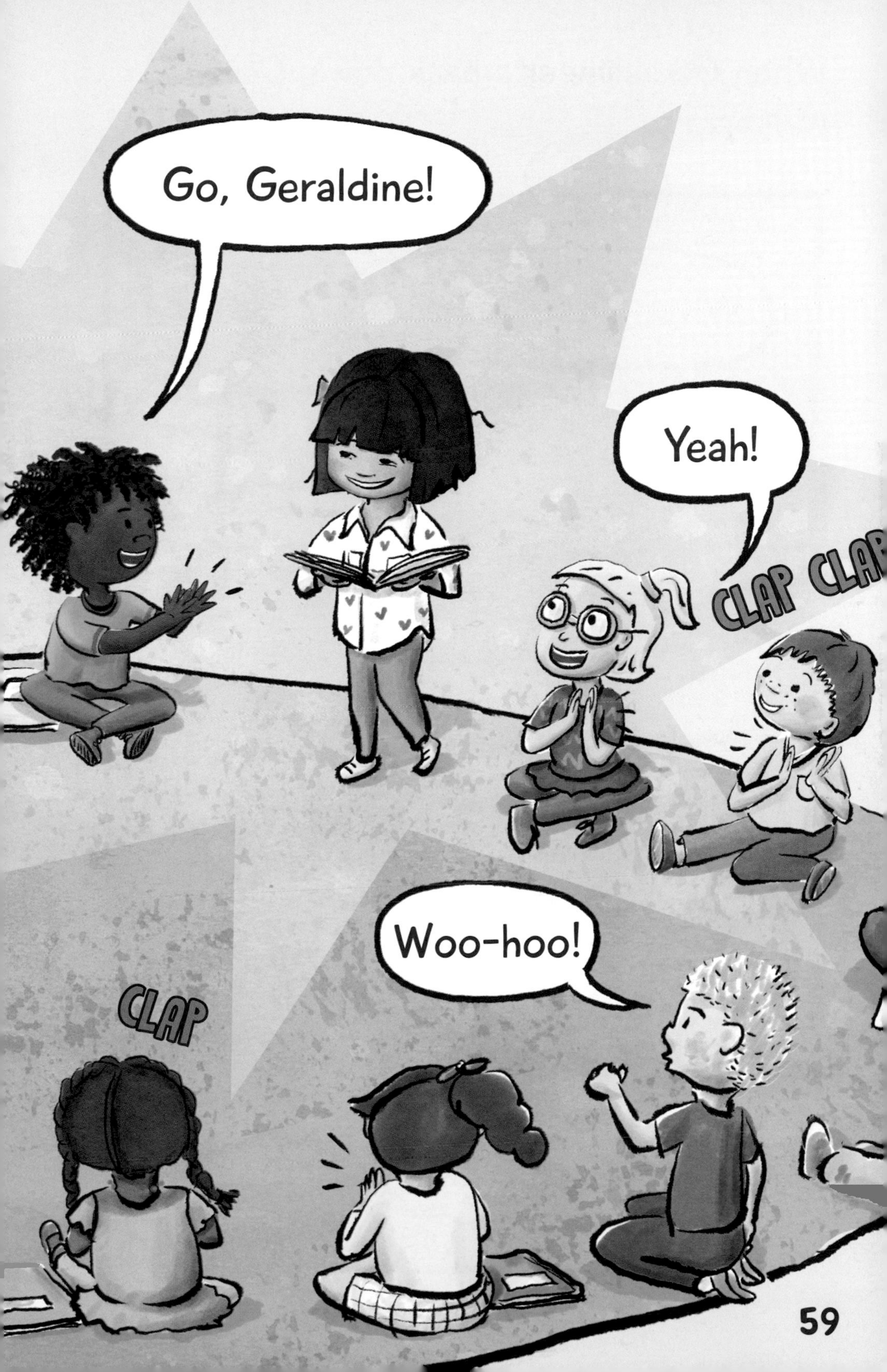
Go, Geraldine!
Yeah!
CLAP CLAP
Woo-hoo!
CLAP

When Geraldine sits back down, Deven whispers:

The End

A MESSAGE FROM CHIENBEE

Families can come in all different forms—biological, adoptive, foster, or special people like friends and caregivers who love you like family. Learning about your family history helps you understand who you are and where you come from. There's a lot you can discover through photo albums, books, interviewing family members, or researching with them online.

Did you know that your family stories can live on for a really, really, really long time through customs such as storytelling, music, art, and dance? For example: traditional Chinese dance, like the kinds Amah used to perform, tells stories of China's very distant past using movement and music. These dancers often hold something like a fluttering fan or whirling ribbons. Isn't it incredible that the costumes and movements performed hundreds of years ago are still around today?

Once you start learning more about your family stories, you will find that you're part of a really big world—a world that's woven together. What will you discover about your family and yourself?

HOW TO MAKE A SCRAPBOOK

A scrapbook is a special book that collects and saves personal stories. It is a fun and creative way to share memories with friends, family, and even future generations. Here's a scrapbook you can make to help you remember special moments.

Step 1. Ask an adult to help you gather supplies:

- glue or tape
- pen or pencil for writing
- printed photos or drawings of your memories
- memorabilia (said like this: meh-muh-ruh-BEE-LEE-uh): paper scraps that remind you of an event or a place, like theater ticket stubs, event flyers and programs, greeting cards, and so on.

- scrapbook album or blank pages that you can staple together

Optional:
- stickers
- crayons, colored pencils, pens, or markers for adding decorations

Step 2. Pick themes for different sections in your scrapbook. Here are some ideas to choose from:

- summer activities
- a holiday you enjoyed
- your birthday
- a trip
- a performance you were in
- a show or movie you attended
- fun with friends

- memories with a pet
- a new experience
- an accomplishment
- favorites of the moment: food, song, book, or school subject
- anything you remember the most from the last year

Step 3. Collect memorabilia and a few pictures for each spread. Your pictures could be photographs or drawings of your memory, or both.

Step 4. Glue or tape down your pictures and memorabilia.

Step 5. Next to the pictures and memorabilia, write a caption that explains what they are and what they mean to you.

Step 6. If you'd like, decorate your pages with stickers and doodles.

Step 7. Have fun sharing your scrapbook with your friends and family!